FIRST

भारत INDIA

OM R2

INDIA R13

CRICKET

R23

भारत INDIA

FIRST-CLASS MAIL
INTERNATIONAL

भारत INDIA R17

FESTIVAL OF LIGHTS
DIWALI

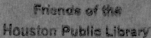

भारत INDIA R

TAJ MAHAL

भारत INDIA R8

MAHATMA GANDHI

भारत INDIA

LOTUS 7r

INDIA R7

FOOTBALL

भारत

COBRA INDIA

INDIA R33 भारत

Peacock

AIR MAIL

Sarod

भारत
INDIA

R5

a giant Thank You to
Sunshine School,
my didi Renee,
Mom + Dad,
and
my Book Guru,
Christy O.
Dhanyavad!

for
Tulsi
and Patrick

Henry Holt and Company, LLC, *Publishers since 1866*
175 Fifth Avenue, New York, New York 10010
mackids.com

Henry Holt® is a registered trademark of Henry Holt and Company, LLC.

Library of Congress Cataloging-in-Publication Data
Kostecki-Shaw, Jenny Sue.
Same, same but different / by Jenny Sue Kostecki-Shaw. — 1st ed.
      p.   cm.
"Christy Ottaviano books."

Summary: Pen pals Elliott and Kailash discover that even though
they live in different countries—America and India—they both
love to climb trees, own pets, and ride school buses.

ISBN 978-0-8050-8946-2
[1. Pen pals—Fiction. 2. Friendship—Fiction.] I. Title.
PZ7.K85278Sam 2011   [E]—dc22   2010030121

First Edition—2011 / Designed by Jenny Sue Kostecki-Shaw and April Ward
The artist used acrylics, crayon, pencil, collage, and tissue paper on Strathmore
illustration board to create the illustrations for this book.
Printed in the United States of America by Lehigh Phoenix,
Rockaway, New Jersey

3 5 7 9 10 8 6 4 2

SAME, SAME but DIFFERENT

Jenny Sue Kostecki-Shaw

Christy Ottaviano Books
Henry Holt and Company • New York

In art class, I painted a picture of my world.
My teacher mailed it across the oceans.

A boy drew back with colors of the sea.

This is my world.
is my world.
Same, same but different.

INDIA
R1

P.S. Who are you?

My name is Kailash, and I love to climb trees too. Same, same but different!

This is me. →

P.S. Do you live in a tree?

That is my tree house where I play. I live in a red brick building with my mom, dad, and baby sister.

I live with my family too—all twenty-three of us—
my mom, dad, sister, brother, grandmother,
grandfather, aunties, uncles, cousins . . .

and our animals.

I have pets too, but not
nearly as many as you!

Same, same but different!

P.S. What does it look
like where you live?

e.

A great river flows through my village.

Peacocks dance under trees shaped like umbrellas.

The sun is **giant** and especially hot here.

In my city, the sun hides behind buildings as **tall** as the sky.

Taxis,
buses,
and cars
fill
the streets.

Here, there are few cars and still too much traffic. Same, same but different!

SHIVA'S HAIR SALOON

PURE VEG
SOUTH INDIAN THALI & DOSAS

खाद्दि
मिठाई

AMAN'S TIP-TOP
Service Center
Parle-G

हनुमान चाय
HANUMAN TEA

KRISHNA
MILK
SWEET

me →

SUNSHINE SCHOOL

So do I!
Same, same
but different!

This is OUR alphabet.

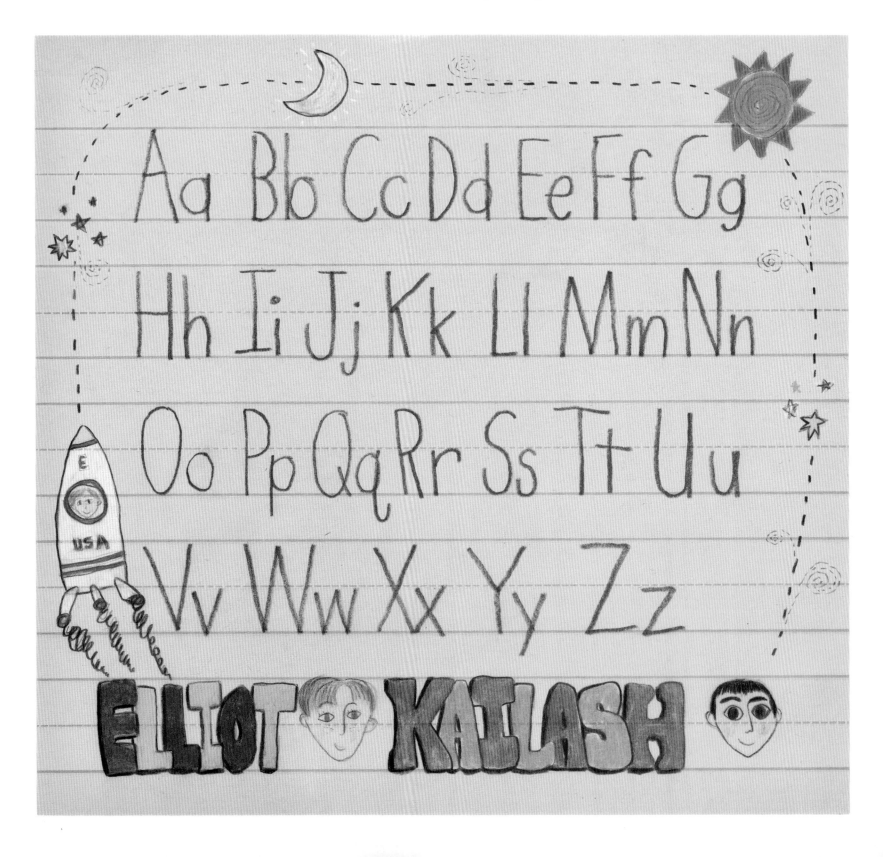

My favorite class is art, where I can be anything.

e.

My favorite class is **yoga**, where I can be anything. Same, same but different!

This is how my friends and I say **hello.**

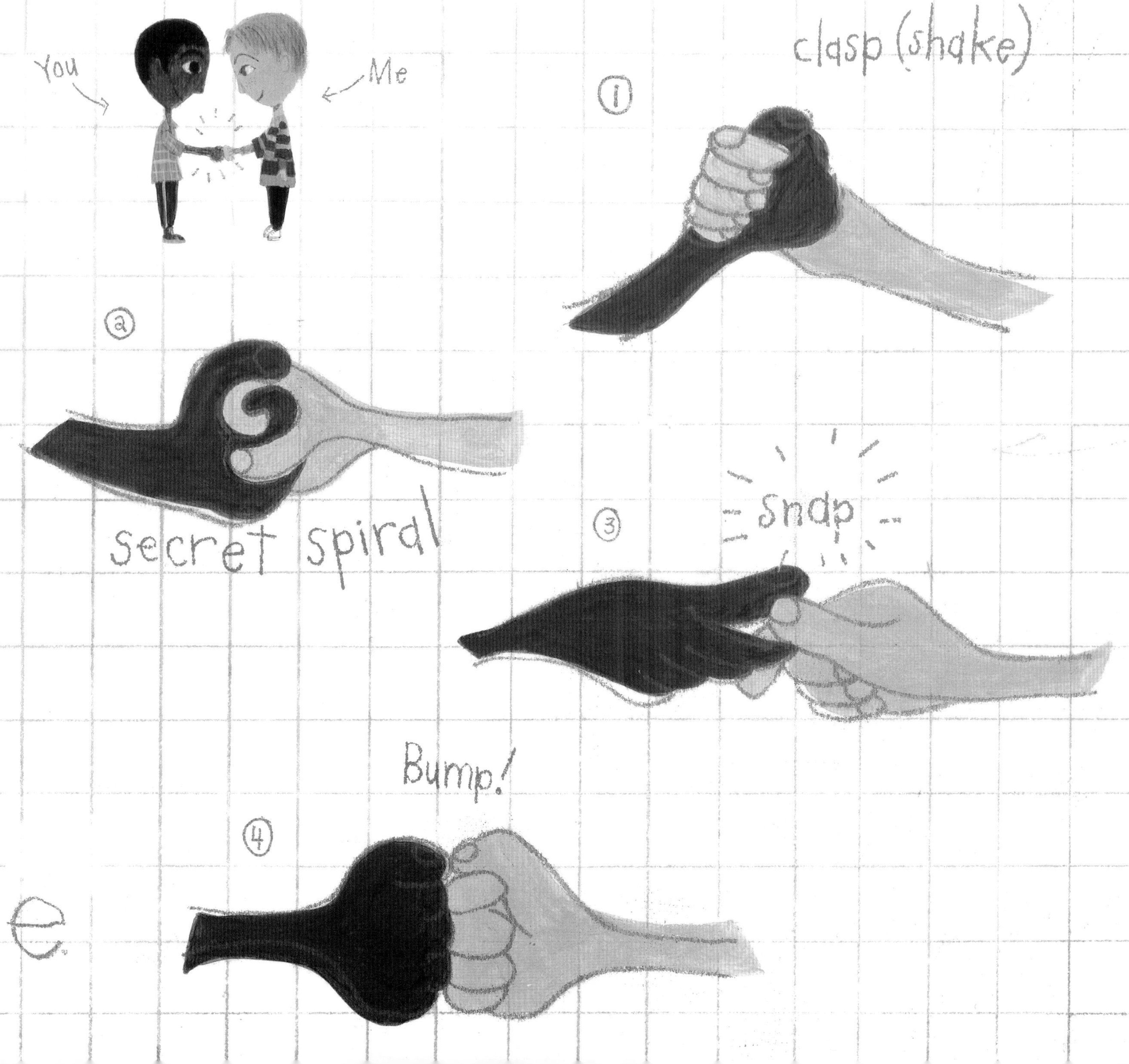

You →

← Me

clasp (shake)

①

② secret spiral

③ Snap

Bump!

④

This is how
my friends and I
say
hello.

you →

← me

NAMASTE नमस्ते

Same, same but different!

K

We're best friends . . .

even though we live in
two different worlds.

Or do we?

This is my world.
Same, same but different!

P.S. Who are you?

My name is Kailash,
and I love to climb trees too. Same, same but different!

This
is me

P.S. Do you live in a tree?

I live with my family too—all twenty-three of us—
my mom, dad, sister, brother, grandmother,
grandfather, aunties, uncles, cousins . . .

and our animals.

A great river flows through my village.

Peacocks dance under trees shaped like umbrellas.

The sun is
giant and
especially hot here.

Here there are
few cars and still
too much traffic.
Same, same
but different!

PURE VEG

So do I!
Same, same
but different!

My
favorite
class is
yoga,
where
I can be
anything.
Same, same
but
different!

This is our alphabet.

Kailash → कैलाश
Elliot,
एलिअट

Same, same but different!

This is how
my friends and I
say
hello.

NAMASTE नमस्ते

Same, same but different!

This is my world.

My name is Elliot, and I love to climb trees.

That is my tree house where I play. I live in a red brick building with my mom, dad, and baby sister.

I ride a bus to school with my friends.

I have pets too, but not nearly as many as you!

Same, same but different!

P.S. What does it look like where you live?

In my city, the sun hides behind buildings as tall as the sky.

Taxis, buses, and cars fill the streets.

My favorite class is art, where I can be anything.

This is OUR alphabet.

Aa Bb Cc Dd Ee Ff Gg
Hh Ii Jj Kk Ll Mm Nn
Oo Pp Qq Rr Ss Tt Uu
Vv Ww Xx Yy Zz

ELLIOT KAILASH

Different, different

but the SAME!

peace

FIRST-CLASS INTERNAT

BASEBALL · 42 USA

FIRST CLASS MAIL

SPECIAL DELIVERY

USA 98

35 MERRY CHRISTMAS · USA

J9 USA · STATUE of LIBERTY

63¢ USA · MARTIN LUTHER KING JR

USA 32 · SOCCER

FIRST-CLASS INTERNATI

1¢ · USA · RATTLESNAKE

USA 23 · ROCK·N·ROLL

FIRST CLASS

BALD EAGLE · 39 USA